AR: L-4.1/P-0.5

Big-Air Snowboarding

by Anne T. McKenna

Consultant:

Don Sather

United States of America Snowboard Association

(USASA)

CAPSTONE
HIGH-INTEREST
BOOKS

an imprint of Capstone Press
Mankato, Minnesota

Capstone High-Interest Books are published by Capstone Press
151 Good Counsel Drive, P.O. Box 669, Mankato, Minnesota 56002
http://www.capstone-press.com

Library of Congress Cataloging-in-Publication Data
McKenna, A. T.
Big-air snowboarding/Anne T. McKenna.
p. cm.—(Extreme sports)
Includes bibliographical references (p. 45) and index.
Summary: Describes the history, equipment, techniques, and safety
measures of big-air snowboarding.
ISBN 0-7368-0166-9
1. Snowboarding—Juvenile literature. [1. Snowboarding.] I. Title.
II. Series.
GV857.S57M364 1999
796.9—dc21
                                                                98-45515
                                                                     CIP
                                                                      AC

Editorial Credits
Matt Doeden, editor; Timothy Halldin, cover designer; Sheri Gosewisch
and Kimberly Danger, photo researchers

Photo Credits
Eric Sanford/Tom Stack & Associates, 31
Index Stock Imagery, cover, 4; Index Stock Imagery and Don Cudney, 7;
    Randy Klamm, 21; Todd Powell, 38
International Stock/Eric Sanford, 16; Tony Demin, 34–35
Mark Turner, 26
Morrow Snowboards, 18, 25
Patrick Batchelder, 28
PhotoBank, Inc./James W. Kay, 33, 36, 43
Photophile/Keith Edwards, 40
Sherman Poppen, 12, 14
Stephen Ingram, 8
Todd W. Patrick, 11
Tom Stack & Associates, 22

2 3 4 5 6 05 04 03 02

Table of Contents

Chapter 1   Big-Air Snowboarding.................. 5

Chapter 2   History of Snowboarding........... 13

Chapter 3   Big-Air Competition 19

Chapter 4   Equipment 27

Chapter 5   Snowboarding Safety................. 37

Features

Photo Diagram 34

Words to Know 44

To Learn More 45

Useful Addresses 46

Internet Sites..................................... 47

Index 48

Chapter 1
Big-Air Snowboarding

The sport of snowboarding is a combination of surfing and skiing. Snowboarders ride snowboards that are shaped like surfboards. Snowboarders balance on these snowboards and speed down snow-covered slopes.

Big-air snowboarding is one popular form of snowboarding. Big-air snowboarders take long jumps into the air on their boards. They do tricks such as flips and spins while they are in the air.

Big-air snowboarders perform tricks in the air.

Catching Air

Snowboarders sometimes take long or high jumps into the air. They call this "catching air" or "catching big air." Snowboarders catch big air in two main ways. They catch big air by riding over drop-offs or by going off jumps.

Drop-offs are areas where slopes suddenly become steep. Snowboarders speed down slopes toward drop-offs. They soar into the air when they go over the drop-offs. Extreme big-air riders sometimes use cliffs as drop-offs. The cliff drop-offs may be 60 feet (18 meters) or more straight down.

Jumps can be natural snow formations or ramps that people have built. Some snowboarders use ski ramps as jumps. Jumps often are more than 100 feet (30 meters) high. They can be close to 400 feet (122 meters) long.

Jumps and Landings

Snowboarders must build up speed before they can catch air. They begin at the top of a slope.

Snowboarders catch big air off jumps and drop-offs.

They speed down the slope until they hit the drop-off or the jump. They go fast so they can stay in the air longer. Then, they can do better tricks.

Snowboarders must keep their rides smooth while they are in the air. They hold their arms out to their sides to balance themselves. They center their weight on their boards. This helps them ride and land smoothly.

Landing can be dangerous for big-air snowboarders. Snowboarders who catch big air travel fast. They could be hurt if they fall during landings.

Terrain Parks

Some ski areas have special places for snowboarders. These areas are called terrain parks. Terrain parks have jumps on which big-air snowboarders can practice. They also may have rail slides. Rail slides are objects on which snowboarders slide their boards. Practicing on rail slides helps to develop snowboarders' balance.

Some ski areas have special places for snowboarders.

Some snowboarders create their own snowboarding areas. They find wide slopes that have natural jumps. Sometimes they have to make jumps out of the snow. Snowboarders may bring objects such as logs to the slopes. They use these objects as rail slides.

Half-pipes

Half-pipes are long snow paths with high walls and rounded sides. Snowboarders race up and down the sides of half-pipes. They ride their boards up and off the walls to catch air. They perform tricks while they are in the air. Many snowboarders practice on half-pipes until they are ready to do big-air tricks.

Many ski areas have small half-pipes called mini-pipes for beginning snowboarders. Mini-pipes look like half-pipes, but they are smaller. Beginning riders learn basic tricks on mini-pipes.

Snowboarders use half-pipe walls to catch air.

Chapter 2
History of Snowboarding

Snowboarding began in the mid-1960s when Sherman Poppen invented the first snowboard. Poppen made his board by screwing two skis together with wooden pegs. He gave the board to his daughter. Poppen's wife called the board the Snurfer by combining the words snow and surfer.

Poppen's Snurfer became popular with children in his neighborhood. He wanted to build more Snurfers so more children could

Snurfers were the first snowboards.

buy them. Poppen got a manufacturing company called the Brunswick Corporation to build his boards. These Snurfers were single boards with ropes attached to the fronts. Riders held the ropes for balance.

The Snurfers became very popular in the late 1960s. Snurfer competitions also became popular. Riders from all over the country took part in Snurfer races. One rider was Jake Burton.

In 1979, Burton changed the Snurfer. He put a set of rubber straps on his Snurfer. The rubber straps held the board to his feet.

Officials did not allow Burton to use this Snurfer in

Jake Burton added rubber straps to the Snurfer.

regular competitions. Instead, they created a new kind of Snurfer competition. They called it the open class. Riders could change their Snurfers in any way they wanted for open-class competitions.

The First Snowboards

Burton and another rider named Tom Sims were among the first people to change their Snurfers. They called these new boards snowboards. Snowboards were wider than Snurfers. They had straps to hold the feet. They did not have ropes attached to their front ends.

Sims and Burton started their own snowboard companies. These companies are two of the top snowboard companies today. Sims called his company Sims Snowboards. Burton called his company Burton Snowboards.

People used snowboards in competition for the first time in 1980. Sims and Burton competed in this event at Ski Cooper near

Jake Burton started his own snowboard company.

Leadville, Colorado. In 1982, Sims organized the first National Snowboarding Championship. In 1983, Burton started snowboarding's U.S. Open event. Snowboarders from around the world competed in this event. The sport's popularity quickly grew.

Big-Air Snowboarding

In the 1990s, some snowboarders began practicing big-air tricks. They invented difficult tricks to do in the air. The U.S. Open included its first big-air competition in 1996.

In June 1997, the X-Games in San Diego, California, held a big-air snowboarding competition. The ESPN television network hosted the X-Games. Organizers constructed a big-air ramp for the competition. They made 200 tons (181 metric tons) of snow for the event.

Only 16 snowboarders competed in the 1997 X-Games. Peter Line won the men's competition. Tina Dixon won the women's competition. The sport's popularity continued to grow.

Chapter 3
Big-Air Competition

Today, there are many big-air snowboarding competitions. Some of these are at the X-Games, the United States Extreme Snowboarding Championships, and the World Extreme Championship.

Big-air competitors receive points from judges for each jump. Judges give points for height, tricks, and landings. Snowboarders who stay in the air the longest earn the most

Today, snowboarders take part in many different big-air snowboarding competitions.

points. This is because they can do the most difficult tricks. Snowboarders also receive points for good landings.

Snowboarders always are working to invent new and difficult tricks. There are several basic tricks all big-air snowboarders must be able to do. These tricks include grabs, fakies, and aerial spins.

The Grab

The grab is one of the most basic snowboarding tricks. It is one of the first tricks beginners learn. Experienced snowboarders combine the grab with other tricks.

To perform the grab, snowboarders bend their knees while in the air. They raise their boards as far as they can. This is very important. Snowboarders may lose their balance if they have to reach down too far. Snowboarders reach down and grab any part of the board with one or both hands.

The grab is one of the most basic snowboarding tricks.

Fakie

The fakie is another popular big-air trick. Snowboarders ride backwards to perform fakies. They steer the tails of their boards down the slopes. They turn by changing the direction of the tails.

Many snowboarders can do fakies while still on the ground. Fakies are harder to do in the air. Experienced snowboarders can combine fakies with other tricks such as grabs.

Aerial Spins

Aerial spins are among the most difficult big-air tricks. Snowboarders measure aerial spins in degrees. One half spin equals 180 degrees. Snowboarders call this a "180." A full spin equals 360 degrees. Snowboarders call this a "360." Advanced big-air snowboarders can spin as many as two and one-half times in the air. These spins are

Aerial spins are among the most difficult big-air tricks.

called "900s." A world champion snowboarder named Terje Haakonsen can do a "1080" by spinning around three times.

A 180 is the easiest aerial spin. Riders call this trick "forward to fakie" when riders spin from facing forward to facing backward. They call it "fakie to forward" when riders start riding backward and finish facing forward.

Inverted aerials are aerials that include flips. Riders are upside-down when they do inverted aerials. Snowboarders also call these tricks "inverts."

Landings

Landings are important to big-air competitors. Judges award points for smooth landings. Snowboarders must make sure their tricks are not too difficult. The most difficult tricks involve many flips and spins. These tricks are hard to land.

Snowboarders must be able to land without falling. They keep their bodies and boards straight just before a landing. They bend their

Snowboarders must be able to land without falling.

knees. This softens the contact with the snow when they land.

Poor landings can be dangerous for big-air snowboarders. Snowboarders can be hurt if they fall during landings. Snowboarders who fall rarely win competitions.

Chapter 4
Equipment

Big-air snowboarding requires only a few pieces of special equipment. Snowboarders need only snowboards, boots, and bindings.

Beginning snowboarders often rent their equipment from ski areas. This is because snowboards are very expensive. Renting equipment allows beginners to test different kinds without having to spend a lot of money. They can see which styles of equipment they like best.

Snowboarding equipment includes snowboards, boots, and bindings.

Short snowboards are easier to control in the air than long boards are.

Snowboards

Snowboards are made either of composites or wood cores. Composites are mixtures of strong, light materials. Wood cores are layers of wood glued together.

Snowboards come in many sizes. They range in length from 100 centimeters (40 inches) to 181 centimeters (71 inches).

Manufacturers measure the width of a snowboard at its middle. Most snowboards are 18 centimeters (7 inches) to 25 centimeters (10 inches) wide. Big-air snowboarders usually choose short boards. Short boards are easier to control in the air than long boards are.

Nose and Tail

The front end of a snowboard is called the nose or tip. The nose curls up slightly at the end. This helps the board glide easily over snow. The snowboard's curled nose keeps it from becoming stuck in hard snow.

The back end of the snowboard is the tail. The tail also is curled. This is so the board does not stick in the snow when the snowboarder lands or rides fakie.

Choosing a Board

Snowboarders should choose their boards carefully. They should choose boards based on their own height and weight. Taller and heavier snowboarders need longer and wider snowboards. These larger boards help the snowboarders keep their balance.

Most big-air snowboarders use freestyle snowboards. These boards are wide and short. They also are flexible. Riders can do more tricks in the air with flexible snowboards. Boards that are not flexible do not move as easily through the air.

Some beginning snowboarders start with freestyle boards. Others start with freeride boards. Freeride boards are less flexible than freestyle boards. They are easier to control when riding fast on the snow.

A beginning snowboarder should choose a board by holding it upright. The tail should be on the ground. The board's nose should come somewhere between the snowboarder's shoulder and nose. Experienced snowboarders and workers at snowboard shops can help beginners select boards.

Big-air snowboarders do not select their boards this way. They usually choose shorter boards. The shorter boards are easier to

Snowboard boots support boarders' ankles.

control in the air. Beginners should not select
boards this way.

Boots

Snowboard boots support snowboarders'
ankles. Boots usually are made of leather,
rubber, and waterproof materials. They have
laces in the front. Snowboarders rarely use ski

boots with their snowboards. Ski boots are made differently than snowboard boots. They are not flexible enough for snowboarders.

There are two types of snowboard boots. They are soft boots and hard boots. Big-air snowboarders use soft boots. Soft boots are light and flexible. They allow snowboarders to move their ankles. Big-air snowboarders must be able to move their ankles to perform tricks. Hard boots prevent them from doing this.

Bindings

Bindings hold the boots to the snowboard. Bindings can be made of metal, plastic, composites, or a mix of the three. Plastic bindings are flexible. This allows big-air snowboarders to do difficult tricks. But plastic bindings may become brittle in the cold and break. Metal and composite bindings are less flexible than plastic bindings. But they do not break as easily.

There are two main kinds of bindings. They are freestyle and step-in bindings. Freestyle

Bindings hold the boots to the snowboard.

bindings give good flexibility. Freestyle bindings have two straps that go over the foot. One strap holds the heel down. The other strap holds the toe down.

Step-in bindings are a newer kind of binding. They allow snowboarders to step into the bindings without the need to attach straps. Snowboard boots are made to fit into step-in bindings.

Goggles

Glove

Tail

Bindings

Nose

Chapter 5
Snowboarding Safety

Big-air snowboarding can be dangerous.
Snowboarders may go very fast before
they jump. They may jump high and far.
Snowboarders can be hurt easily if they do
not land properly. Snowboarders have special
clothing and equipment to help protect them
from the dangers of snowboarding.

Big-air snowboarding can be dangerous.

Outer layers of snowboarding clothing must be waterproof and windproof.

Clothing

Snowboard clothing must be warm and dry. It must protect snowboarders from cold weather. It also must keep wet snow away from their skin. Outer layers of clothing should be waterproof and windproof. This will keep snowboarders warm and dry.

Snowboard clothing should fit loosely enough to allow snowboarders freedom to move. Loose clothing also allows snowboarders to wear many layers of clothing. When the weather is cold, snowboarders wear several layers of clothing under their outer layer. The layers of clothing provide both warmth and protection. Snowboarders can take layers off if they become too warm.

Gloves, Hats, and Goggles

Snowboarders wear gloves to protect their hands. Snowboarding gloves should be waterproof to keep the hands dry. Gloves also should have tight material around the wrists to keep out snow.

Snowboarders should wear hats during cold weather. People without hats can lose much of their body heat through their heads. Hats also can keep the wind out of snowboarders' ears. Hats should be tight enough that they will not fall off during rides.

Goggles protect snowboarders' eyes.

Goggles protect snowboarders' eyes from snow, wind, and the sun. Goggles also protect snowboarders' faces during falls.

Other Safety Measures

Snowboarders' boots sometimes release from their bindings during a fall. Snowboarders use safety leashes to keep their boards with them at all times. Safety leashes are small straps that attach to snowboards and snowboarders. The leashes keep snowboards from slipping away when riders put them on and take them off. Safety leashes prevent boards from hitting other people. They also prevent snowboarders from losing their boards.

Snowboarders also wear sunblock. Snow can reflect up to 90 percent of the sun's rays. These rays can burn the skin even during winter. Snowboarders can become badly sunburned if they do not wear sunblock.

Cold-Weather Dangers

Heat packs keep snowboarders' feet and hands warm on very cold days. Snowboarders could get frostbite without heat packs. Frostbite occurs when cold air freezes uncovered skin or skin next to wet clothing.

Snowboarders may suffer from hypothermia if they become too cold. This means the body temperature becomes too low. One way snowboarders avoid hypothermia is by eating well before snowboarding. Eating well supplies snowboarders' bodies with extra energy to stay warm. Waterproof clothing also helps prevent hypothermia. People become cold faster when they are wet.

Snowboarders must drink plenty of water before snowboarding. They may become dehydrated if they do not have enough water in their bodies.

Boarder Patrol

Many ski areas have boarder patrol units. Members of these units watch slopes for snowboarders who are hurt. They help anyone who is in trouble.

Members of boarder patrol units must pass a series of tests. They must be strong and alert. They also must be good snowboarders.

Some boarder patrol members watch for snowboarders who are not riding safely. The patrol members ask these snowboarders to leave ski parks. This helps keep other snowboarders safe.

Snowboarders should always practice in groups.

Big-air snowboarders must also work to keep themselves safe. They should never snowboard alone. They must be sure to have all the proper safety equipment. They must always remember to ride safely. Then, they can enjoy their sport without being hurt or hurting others.

Words to Know

binding (BINDE-ing)—a device that attaches a snowboarder's boot to a snowboard

composite (kuhm-POZ-it)—a mixture of strong, light materials used to make snowboards and bindings

drop-off (DROP-AWF)—an area that suddenly becomes very steep

flexible (FLEK-suh-buhl)—able to bend and move easily

frostbite (FRAWST-bite)—a condition that occurs when cold air freezes uncovered skin or skin next to wet clothing

half-pipe (HAF-pipe)—a U-shaped snow structure built for snowboarders

mini-pipe (MIN-ee-pipe)—a small half-pipe

rail slide (RAYL SLIDE)—an object that snowboarders slide along on their snowboards

terrain park (tuh-RAYN PARK)—an area at a ski park just for snowboarders

To Learn More

Brimner, Larry Dane. *Snowboarding*. A First Book. New York: Franklin Watts, 1997.

Jay, Jackson. *Snowboarding Basics*. New Action Sports. Mankato, Minn.: Capstone Press, 1996.

Kidd, P. J. *Snowboarding: Big Air and Boarder X*. Extreme Games. Edina, Minn.: Abdo & Daughters, 1999.

Lurie, Jon. *Fundamental Snowboarding*. Fundamental Sports. Minneapolis: Lerner Publications, 1996.

Ryan, Pat. *Extreme Snowboarding*. Extreme Sports. Mankato, Minn.: Capstone Press, 1998.

Useful Addresses

American Association of Snowboard Instructors (AASI)
133 South Van Gordon Street
Suite 100
Lakewood, CO 80228

Canadian Snowboard Federation
250 West Beaver Creek Road
Unit One — Second Floor
Richmond Hill, ON L4B 1C7
Canada

Professional Snowboarders Association of North America
P.O. Box 477
Vail, CO 81658

Internet Sites

ESPN.com Extreme Sports
http://espn.go.com/extreme

International Snowboard Federation
http://www.isf.net

Mountain Zone
http://www.mountainzone.com/snowboarding

Snowboarding Online
http://www.solsnowboarding.com

U.S. Amateur Snowboard Association
http://www.usasa.org

Index

aerial spin, 20, 23–24

bindings, 27, 32–33, 40
boarder patrol, 42
boots, 27, 31–32, 33, 40
Burton, Jake, 14, 15, 16

cliffs, 6

Dixon, Tina, 17
drop-off, 6, 9

fakie, 20, 23, 24, 29
frostbite, 41

grab, 20, 23

Haakonsen, Terje, 24
half-pipes, 10
hypothermia, 41–42

Line, Peter, 17

mini-pipes, 10

National Snowboarding
    Championship, 16

Poppen, Sherman, 13, 14

rail slides, 9, 10
ramp, 6, 17

safety leashes, 40–41
Sims, Tom, 15, 16
Snurfer, 13–15
sunblock, 41

terrain parks, 9–10

United States Extreme
    Snowboarding
    Championships, 19
U.S. Open, 16

World Extreme
    Championship, 19

X-Games, 17, 19